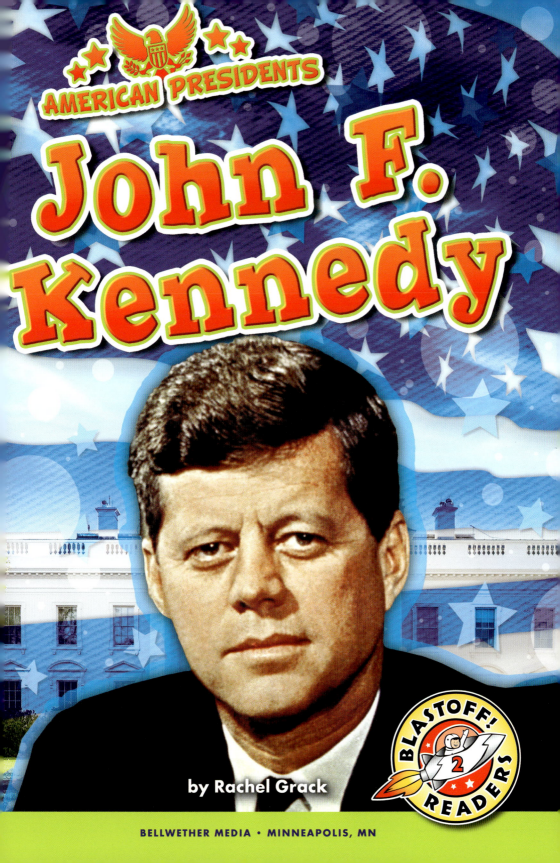

Blastoff! Readers are carefully developed by literacy experts to build reading stamina and move students toward fluency by combining standards-based content with developmentally appropriate text.

 Level 1 provides the most support through repetition of high-frequency words, light text, predictable sentence patterns, and strong visual support.

 Level 2 offers early readers a bit more challenge through varied sentences, increased text load, and text-supportive special features.

 Level 3 advances early-fluent readers toward fluency through increased text load, less reliance on photos, advancing concepts, longer sentences, and more complex special features.

★ **Blastoff! Universe**

This edition first published in 2022 by Bellwether Media, Inc.

No part of this publication may be reproduced in whole or in part without written permission of the publisher. For information regarding permission, write to Bellwether Media, Inc., Attention: Permissions Department, 6012 Blue Circle Drive, Minnetonka, MN 55343.

Library of Congress Cataloging-in-Publication Data

Names: Koestler-Grack, Rachel A., 1973- author.
Title: John F. Kennedy / by Rachel Grack.
Description: Minneapolis, MN : Bellwether Media, Inc., 2022. | Series: Blastoff! Readers: American Presidents | Includes bibliographical references and index. | Audience: Ages 5-8 | Audience: Grades 2-3 | Summary: "Relevant images match informative text in this introduction to John F. Kennedy. Intended for students in kindergarten through third grade"-- Provided by publisher.
Identifiers: LCCN 2021011405 (print) | LCCN 2021011406 (ebook) | ISBN 9781644875179 (library binding) | ISBN 9781648344855 (paperback) | ISBN 9781648344251 (ebook)
Subjects: LCSH: Kennedy, John F. (John Fitzgerald), 1917-1963--Juvenile literature. | Presidents--United States--Biography--Juvenile literature.
Classification: LCC E842.Z9 K64 2022 (print) | LCC E842.Z9 (ebook) | DDC 973.922092 [B]--dc23
LC record available at https://lccn.loc.gov/2021011405
LC ebook record available at https://lccn.loc.gov/2021011406

Text copyright © 2022 by Bellwether Media, Inc. BLASTOFF! READERS and associated logos are trademarks and/or registered trademarks of Bellwether Media, Inc.

Editor: Elizabeth Neuenfeldt   Designer: Josh Brink

Printed in the United States of America, North Mankato, MN.

Table of Contents

Who Was John F. Kennedy?	4
Time in Office	12
What John Left Behind	20
Glossary	22
To Learn More	23
Index	24

Who Was John F. Kennedy?

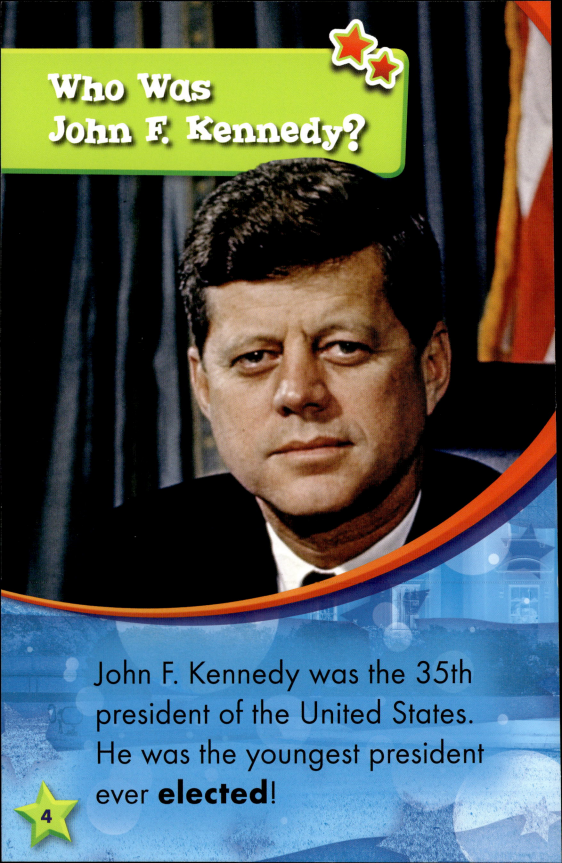

John F. Kennedy was the 35th president of the United States. He was the youngest president ever **elected**!

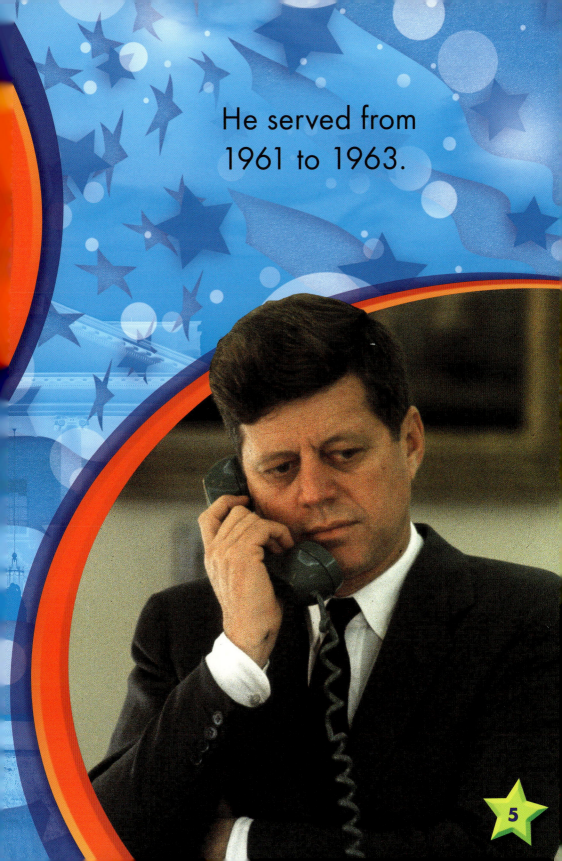

He served from 1961 to 1963.

John's Hometown

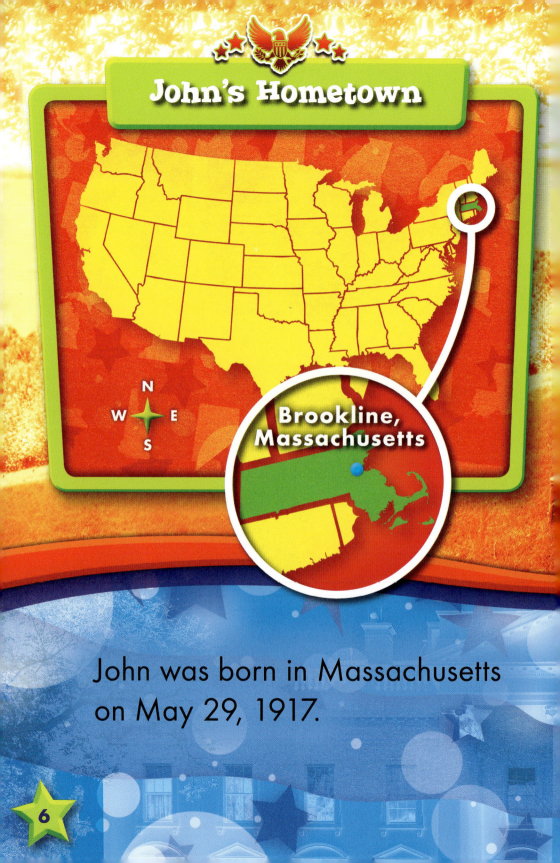

John was born in Massachusetts on May 29, 1917.

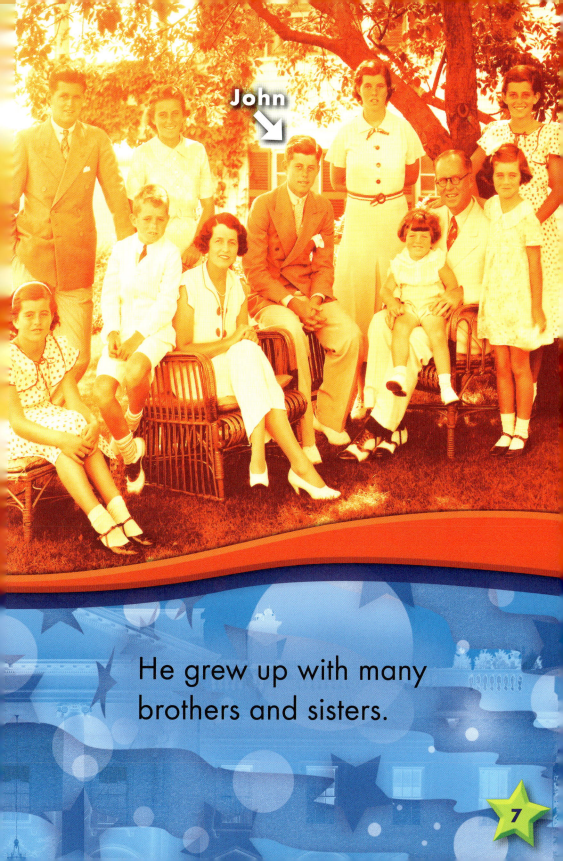

He grew up with many brothers and sisters.

John studied government at Harvard. One of his papers became a popular book.

Presidential Picks

Books

Peter Pan and *The Price of Union*

Sports

golf, sailing, swimming, and tennis

Food

soup

Music

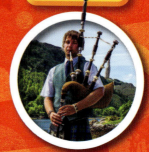

jazz and bagpipes

John in World War II, 1942

Later, he joined the U.S. Navy. He served in **World War II**. He was a hero!

After the war, John ran for the **House of Representatives**. He served for six years.

In 1952, he was elected as a **senator**.

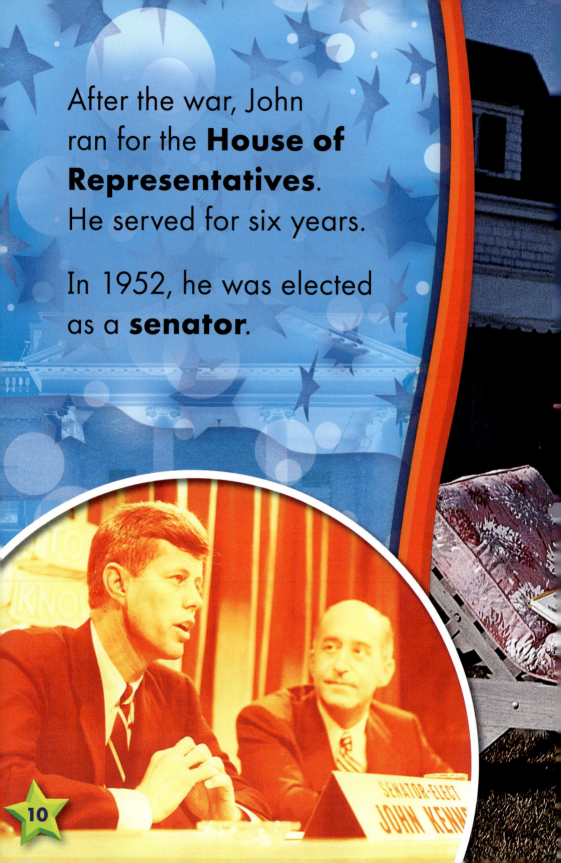

Question

How did John's early life help him become president?

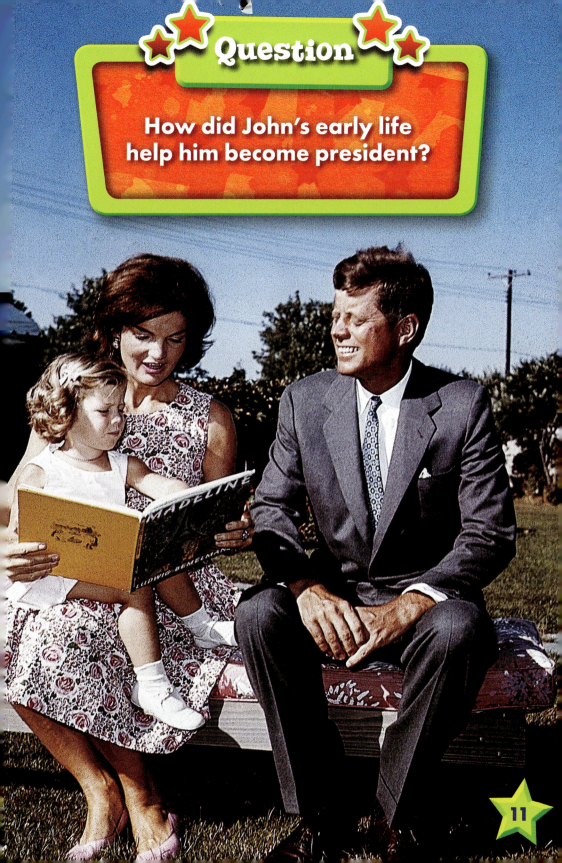

Time in Office

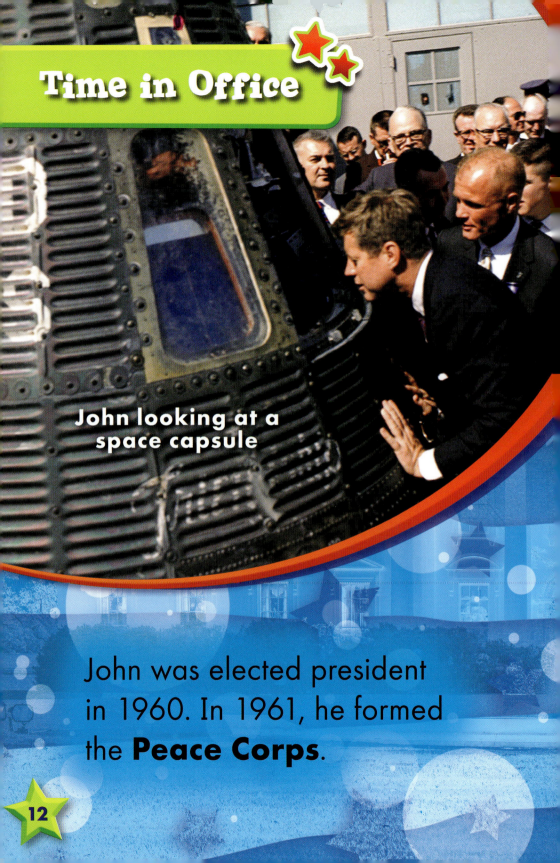

John looking at a space capsule

John was elected president in 1960. In 1961, he formed the **Peace Corps**.

He also strengthened the space **program**. He wanted the U.S. to reach the moon first!

Presidential Profile

Place of Birth
Brookline, Massachusetts

Birthday
May 29, 1917

Schooling
Harvard University

Term
1961 to 1963

Party
Democratic

Signature

Vice President
Lyndon B. Johnson

John was president during the **Cold War**. In 1962, **nuclear war** nearly broke out.

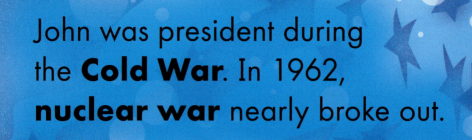

John with the leader of the former Soviet Union

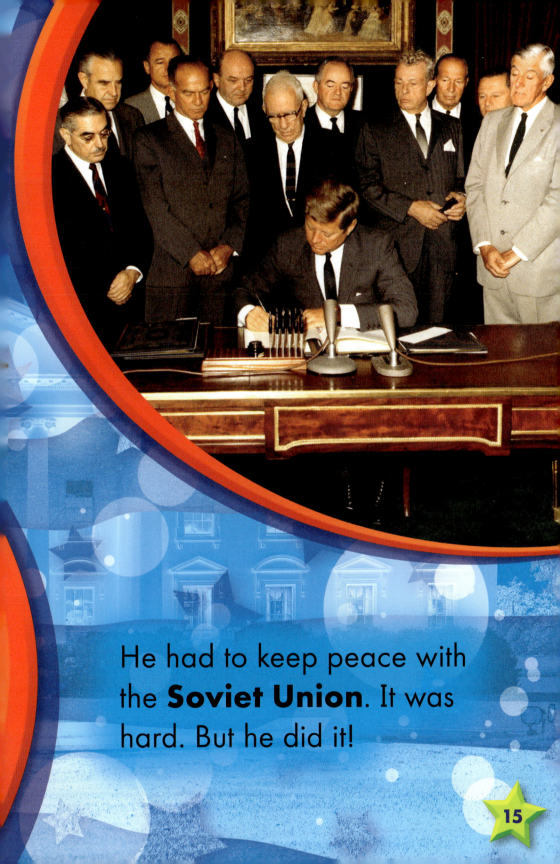

He had to keep peace with the **Soviet Union**. It was hard. But he did it!

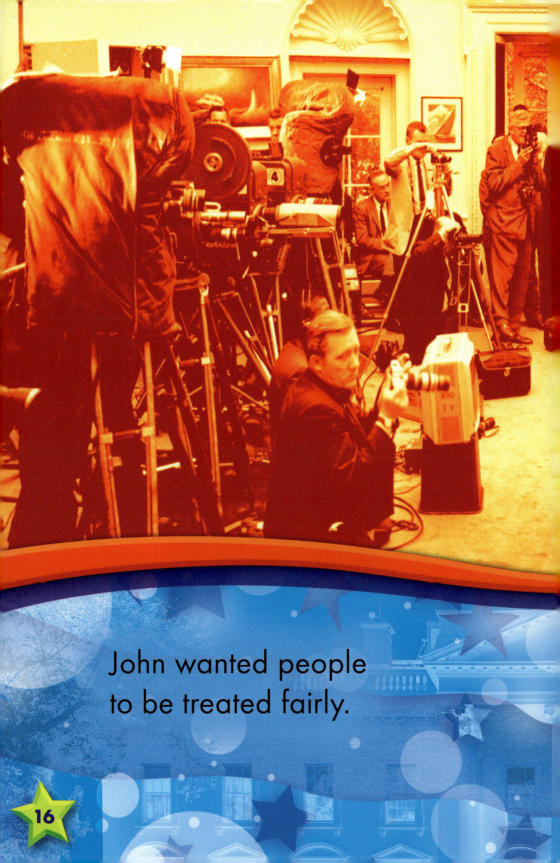

John wanted people to be treated fairly.

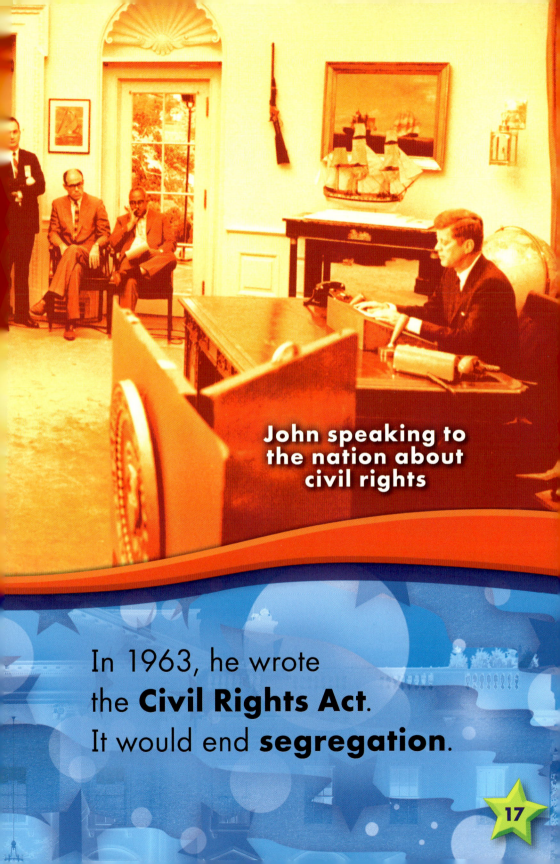

John speaking to the nation about civil rights

In 1963, he wrote the **Civil Rights Act**. It would end **segregation**.

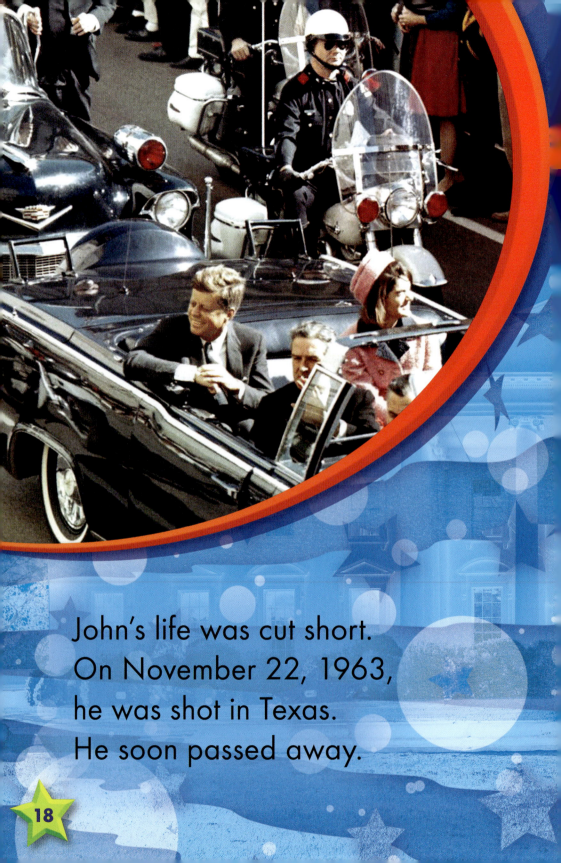

John's life was cut short.
On November 22, 1963,
he was shot in Texas.
He soon passed away.

John Timeline

November 8, 1960
John F. Kennedy is elected president

March 1, 1961
John forms the Peace Corps

October 1962
Nuclear war almost breaks out

November 22, 1963
John dies

July 2, 1964
The Civil Rights Act is passed

July 20, 1969
The U.S. is the first country to land on the moon

What John Left Behind

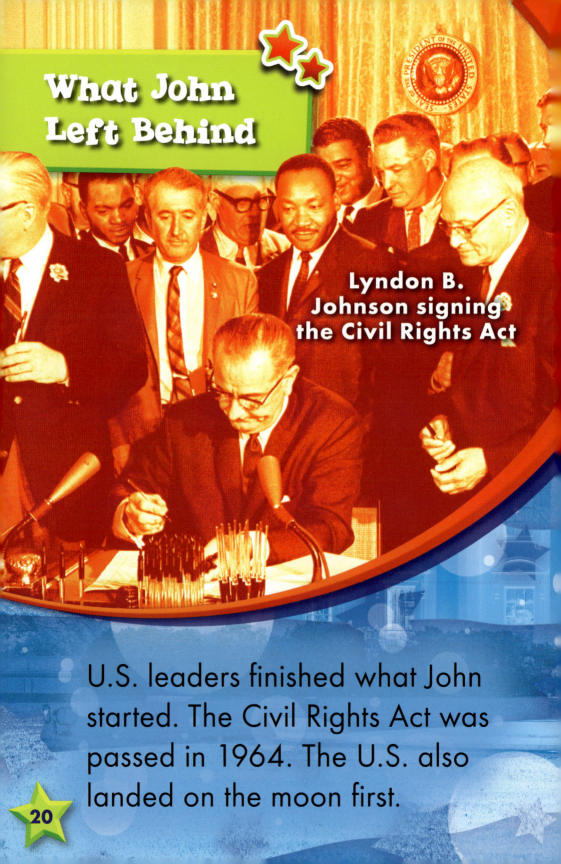

Lyndon B. Johnson signing the Civil Rights Act

U.S. leaders finished what John started. The Civil Rights Act was passed in 1964. The U.S. also landed on the moon first.

John's leadership **inspired** many people!

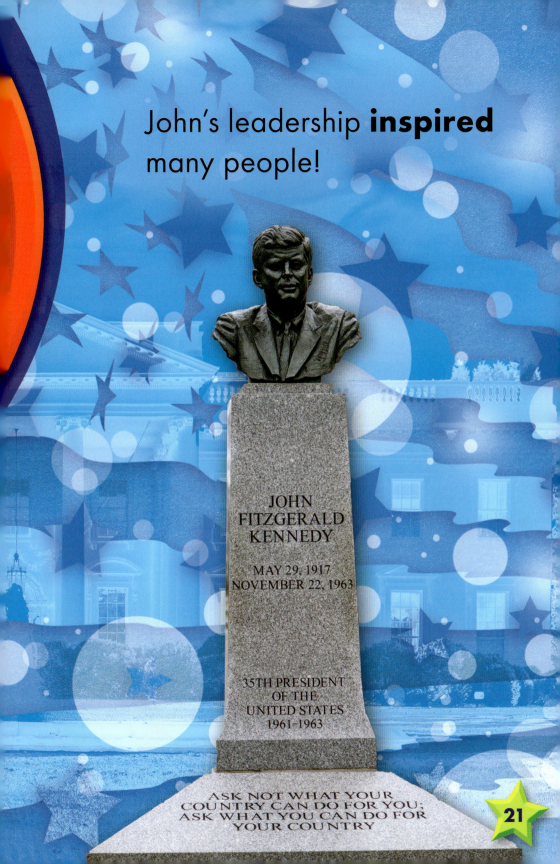

Glossary

Civil Rights Act—a law passed in 1964 that states people cannot be treated unfairly because of their race, gender, religion, or home country; it also ended segregation across the U.S.

Cold War—the conflict between the U.S. and the Soviet Union in the second half of the 1900s that did not break out into fighting

elected—chosen by voting

House of Representatives—a group of elected people who make laws for the United States

inspired—gave someone an idea about what to do or create

nuclear war—a war in which countries fight each other with nuclear weapons; nuclear weapons are very powerful and very dangerous.

Peace Corps—a part of the U.S. government that sends people to help in struggling countries

program—a plan of goals that need to be done in order to get a certain result

segregation—the act of keeping groups of people apart based on race

senator—a member of the Senate of the U.S. government; the Senate helps make laws.

Soviet Union—a former country in eastern Europe and western Asia that lasted from 1922 to 1991

World War II—the war fought from 1939 to 1945 that involved many countries

To Learn More

AT THE LIBRARY

Keenan, Sheila. *John F. Kennedy the Brave.* New York, N.Y.: HarperCollins Publishers, 2017.

L'Hoër, Claire. *John F. Kennedy.* Translated by Catherine Nolan. New York, N.Y.: Roaring Brook Press, 2019.

Smith, Sherri L. *What Is the Civil Rights Movement?* New York, N.Y.: Penguin Workshop, 2020.

ON THE WEB

FACTSURFER

Factsurfer.com gives you a safe, fun way to find more information.

1. Go to www.factsurfer.com.

2. Enter "John F. Kennedy" into the search box and click 🔍.

3. Select your book cover to see a list of related content.

Index

birthday, 6
Civil Rights Act, 17, 20
Cold War, 14
elected, 4, 10, 12
family, 7
government, 8
Harvard, 8
hometown, 6
House of Representatives, 10
leadership, 20, 21
Massachusetts, 6
moon, 13, 20
nuclear war, 14
peace, 15
Peace Corps, 12
picks, 8
profile, 13
question, 11
segregation, 17
senator, 10
Soviet Union, 14, 15
space program, 13
Texas, 18
timeline, 19
U.S. Navy, 9
World War II, 9, 10

The images in this book are reproduced through the courtesy of: World History Archive/ Alamy, cover; John Lee Lopez/ Wikimedia Commons, p. 3; Alfred Eisenstaedt/ Contributor/ Getty Images, p. 4; Paul Schutzer/ Contributor/ Getty Images, p. 5; Bachrach/ Contributor/ Getty Images, pp. 6-7; vipman, p. 8 (books); Maridav, p. 8 (tennis); Foodio, p. 8 (soup); Gimas, p. 8 (bagpipes); John F. Kennedy Presidential Library and Museum, Boston/ Wikimedia Commons, p. 9; Historical/ Contributor/ Getty Images, p. 10; Bettmann/ Contributor/ Getty Images, pp. 10-11, 14; NASA Photo/ Alamy, p. 12; Arnold Newman, White House Press Office (WHPO)/ Wikimedia Commons, p. 13; Connormah, John F. Kennedy/ Wikimedia Commons, p. 13 (signature); American Photo Archive/ Alamy, p. 15; John F. Kennedy Presidential Library and Museum/ JFK Library, pp. 16-17; Walt Cisco, Dallas Morning News/ Wikimedia Commons, p. 18; U.S. Government/ Wikimedia Commons, p. 19 (Peace Corps); White House Photo/ Alamy, pp. 19 (Civil Rights Act), 20; castleski, p. 19 (moon landing); rblfmr, p. 21; Chrisdorney, p. 23.